NEBULA

MJ. BENITO

Copyright © 2015 Maria J. Benito

All rights reserved.

ISBN: 1508625719
ISBN-13: 978-15086225711

To two of the bravest men I have ever known:

>my dad, a great man
>my son, a great man-to-be

Thanks for believing in me.

CONTENTS

Acknowledgments

Chapter 1   3

Chapter 2   17

Chapter 3   21

Chapter 4   31

Chapter 5   52

I have always believed, and I still believe, that whatever good or bad fortune may come our way we can always give it meaning and transform it into something of value…

…Some of us think holding on makes us strong; but sometimes it is letting go.

-Herman Hesse-

ACKNOWLEDGMENTS

Inspirations is all around us, especially in people that we love and mean a lot to us, that support us and encourage us to move forward and give the best of us or be the best we can be in life.

Thanks to my family and the few but loyal friends that has been with me all the way to make this dream possible.

Thanks to someone very special that has changed completely the meaning of this story. I don't need to say more; I know you understand.

CHAPTER 1

"Do you believe in destiny?"
The woman turned around to look at him without releasing her grip from the hand-rail of the bridge.
"I beg your pardon?" -there was a mix of disbelief and surprise in her face.
The man repeated the question as he walked slowly towards her.
"I asked if you believe in destiny".
He had seen her when he came from one end of the bridge and had been watching her for a while. The woman seemed to be lost in her thoughts. She had crossed the protected fence of the bridge and seized the hand-rail with both hands with her back to the bridge and was looking down. Paul didn't know what to do. He didn't want to stop her, although it was clear she was interrupting him, but on the other hand he couldn't just hang around and watch her without doing anything. He didn't want to waste all morning either.

"Stay away. Get away from me. Leave me alone" -she watched him nervously and with distrust as he approached her walking slowly with his hands stuffed in his pockets-. I told you, don't come near me.
He realized the woman was on the verge of hysteria, and could jump any time now. He stopped two meters away from where she was holding tight the hand-rail. He noticed that her knuckles were white due to the strength of her grip.
"Take it easy, I won't try to stop you. I'm not here for that. It would be the opposite, if any" -he said these last words more to himself than to her while he looked down over the rail.
She looked at him with his words still reverberating in her head trying to understand the implications of what he just said.
"What do you mean?" -despite the apprehension and fear, she was intrigued.
The man was still looking down, as if he had forgotten about her. It took a while before he spoke again. When he did, his voice sounded far away; as far as his thoughts seemed to be.
"Perhaps we could jump together. It seems hard to do it alone".
They were over an old bridge that years ago had been used as a railroad, until the new train line was shaped. Since then, this and other similar bridges had been abandoned and were only used by old trains that toured occasionally on those now abandoned railways.
But that happened only in summer. On this cold November morning, that isolated railroad bridge over icy waters of the black river was deserted. The rail trucks,

narrower than those used now, were suitable only for old early last century stem trains; they were made out of wood attached to the rails with nails instead of the current concrete beams fixed with thick screws. On each side of the bridge, few rusted railings protected the train from some fifty meters fall above violent and icy waters flowing down.

Tourists were astonished at the lewd sight spotted when crossing the bridge, which seemed to be suspended between the mountains covered with blooming flora in summer. At that time of the year, the visitors felt invited to duck in the crystal clear waters of the limpid river.

But that happened in other times and other circumstances. It happened when the echo returned cheerful voices and laughter from tourists delighted to hear their own voices amplified by the reverberation of the nearby mountains.

The man and the woman standing now on the bridge were not tourists. They hadn't come to enjoy the scenery. They weren't there to appreciate the magnificent view that nature provided. The echo wouldn't return their laughter and their joyful voices.

They were there with a darker purpose: to get rid of their ghosts once and for all; to put an end to suffering and loneliness; to free their souls from emotional despair and painful agony that nested inside.

Two bodies about to be shut down they were; two hearts about to stop beating. They wouldn't feel the sun on the skin, or hear the birds singing in a spring morning, or experience the invigorating rain on the face in a warm summer evening. They wouldn't be there neither to contemplate the beauty of the world, nor to feel anger or suffering the deep desolation that undermined their spirit every day.

"I think we both have had the same idea" -he shrugged while he took off the hands from the pants pockets and held onto the hand-rail.

"You've come to jump?" -She seemed surprised, but reacted immediately with an unusual fury- "who said I'm gonna jump?"

"Sorry mate; my mistake. You were going to bungee jumping, then?" -he was amused by the denial of the evidence she was trying so hard-. "Well, you've been very lucky then as I've decided to skip today and noticed you've forgotten hooking to safety ropes" -he said in a sarcastic humorous tone-. "I would lend you mine; in fact, I would give them away since I won't need them anymore, but unfortunately I haven't brought them with me today".

"Are you really going to jump?" -the woman seemed concerned.

"Are you?"

They looked at each other intensely seeking the missing piece for neither one of them wanted to give up first. Finally, she answered the question.

"Yes, that's what I'm here for" -she seemed determined, although frightened.

He didn't took his eyes from hers.

"Are you afraid?" -the question surprised him more than her.

The woman hesitated before replying.

"A bit maybe" -she looked down again-. "But it can't be worse than keep going, living every day, one day after another. It'll be only a moment, and then everything will be over".

The man also lined out of the hand-rail and peeped down.

"The water seems to be very cold and dark. Can you swim?"

She pondered the question, and replied after a few moments.

"I don't think this really matter. I've been reading, you know. Falling from this height will leave you breathless, and the cold waters will do the rest. I think it will last only a moment. Apparently you lose the conscience rather quickly". -Then, recalling his earlier question, she added- "I can't swim, though".

"I do" -he said speaking to himself-. "I wonder if that matters. Perhaps as you say, the lack of air and hypothermia finish me, but I hadn't thought about the chance of survival. I didn't remember the river".

"Do you think you could survive jumping from that height?" -She seemed interested in that highly remote possibility, for apparently she hadn't thought about it.

"Don't know, but I wouldn't like to jump if it was gonna to be useless for my purpose".

"So, you are going to jump".

"That's why I came here".

"Why do you want to jump?" -The woman asked. But she immediately withdrew the question remorsefully -.

"Sorry, forget it. I don't mind; it's none of my business, anyway".

"It's okay. After all, I suppose we could spare a few minutes before we finish the job. Would you like a coffee?"

"That's preposterous. You've brought coffee in these circumstances?" -The built up stress and the absurd situation made her smile-. "Well, you come prepared, no doubt about it".

He also smiled. Coming to that, the situation would have been quite comical if not for the tragic end foreseen.

"I have brought a flask. Have it in the car. I guess it's a difficult habit to give up". -He shrugged his shoulders apologetically but amused-. "Do you fancy a last parting cup? I'm sorry, but I don't have anything stronger".

"Coffee would do nicely, thanks. It's almost like Jesus and his disciples' last supper. *The last Cup*" -there was sarcasm in her voice, but he preferred to ignore the comment. They were both smiling.

"All right then, I'm going to fetch it. You want a hand crossing the fence back inside?"

"No need; I'll do it myself".

"Fine, but don't leave without me. I'll come back straight away" -he winked at her and withdrew his steps towards the end of the bridge where he had come.

She passed the legs over the railing and noticed she was shaking. As he walked away, the woman stared at him wondering his motives to be there. He marched at good pace while the wind churned his black and thick hair. Despite the situation, she couldn't help notice that the man was tall and attractive, in his early forties probably, and with no wedding ring.

She caught herself watching the finger where her own wedding ring should be. She had taken it off only few hours ago and the pale mark was obvious on his ring finger, where it had been all these years. It was childish to have it removed, but for some reason she didn't want it to be lost or taken by someone when they find her body. It had never been removed in nine years, from the moment her husband put it in her finger in the Church where they got married.

He had struggled to put it on at the ceremony. Leo's brother and best man, in charge of collecting the rings, got confused and took the wrong size rings. Leo's wedding ring danced in his finger, while she barely could fit the band in hers.

"Well, it's no likely that you are gonna lose it or take it off to pretend you're a single woman" -Leo had said in a whisper winking at her and looking at the funny side of the situation. He didn't seem to care too much for the embarrassment of her future brother-in-law while they exchanged the wedding rings at the ceremony.

She smiled now reminiscing the past. So handsome he was uniformed with his full military outfit waiting for her in front of the altar, anxiously checking the time in his wristwatch. And how his eyes sparkled when he saw her entering the temple holding her father's arm! She remembered to have crossed the few meters that kept her away from the high altar almost floating, with her beautiful white dress fluttering around her like butterfly's wings. And were butterfly's wings too those that nested in her stomach when she saw him. Then her father gave her to Leo, and her eyes nailed in her husband's and in this moment she knew he was the man for her and he would be for the rest of her life, until death do them part. And now she was going to die.

The images of the past crowded in her eyes. She recalled the difficult times they had had together, the troubles to pay the rent, to have enough money every month, and then to buy the house when Alba was on the way. She also evoked the happy moments. And there had been very many; countless blissful moments.

They had been dating for two years when they attended the ball held to commemorate Leo's brigade anniversary. She was twenty-two, he twenty-seven. A young and handsome Lieutenant that especially that night shimmered dressed in his finery full uniform. It was the first time for her wearing an evening gown and was very excited.

The Colonel of the regiment and his wife had been very kind to her, as they had said she reminded them of their daughter that was studying abroad, and they were asked to join them at the main table. She enjoyed herself and had the opportunity to talk to some of the very chivalrous Leo's officers and companions. She had a great time.

However, the end of the evening was a surprise to her. They had just arrived to the car and Leo was riled; he had a furious expression. During the entire evening he had been very polite; she thought he had enjoyed as much as her and she couldn't understand what had happened to transform the fun into the anger that he seemed to feel now.

"What happens? Why are you so upset?"

"Can't you guess?"

She looked at him trying to find something that she might have done wrong at the party. Perhaps she had said something that made him feel uncomfortable in front of his superiors or colleagues. However, as much as she was trying to remember, could not find anything she would have neither said nor done that could make him feel enraged.

"No, I can't. What have I done to displease you so much?"

"You've bewitched me, that's what you have done -he spoke very serious".

"I beg your pardon?" -she couldn't believe what she just heard. Leo had always behaved like a judicious person, and now she was discovering he was a lunatic or something worse. How was it possible she didn't noticed before?

Then she realized that Leo was teasing her. She smiled mischievously while waiting for the answer.

"Tonight I felt like killing half of my regiment after seeing the way they looked at you and how you smiled at them" -he approached her with a wicked smile on his lips-. "I think we have to do something to fix it".

"What can we do?" -She asked calmly after realizing he was just jealous.

"We have to get married. It's the only way that they will leave you alone and I can get some sleep at night. I am not willing to be compelled to protect you from those impudent scoundrels every time they see you".

"Are you serious?"

"What do you think?"

They were married as soon as she finished Law School and found work as an intern for a law firm in the city.

They rented a small one bedroom apartment in the city center near her work. It had only a tiny kitchen, living room and a bathroom. It was more than enough; it had the space they needed and was low maintenance.

He was out all week and returned on Friday afternoon. She worked at the law firm and waited anxiously for his arrival on weekends to be together. It was not a very conventional marriage, but it suits them for the meantime. They spent the week thinking about each other and when they met tried to recover the wasted time.
Leo hoped to be transferred in a couple of years and get a position closer where he could return home every night, so they could start thinking about starting a family.
However, things never go as planned, and on their first anniversary Leo received the news that he was going to become a dad. He hastened to request the transfer and six months later got it.
They also started to seek a more appropriate home for the baby. It wasn't an easy task to find something within their budget. They spent over two months viewing houses on Saturdays before finding something that they liked and could afford. Both, Leo's and her parents tried to help them economically, but Leo refused to accept any help.
The two-storey house was located in a residential neighborhood; it was big enough and had a south face back garden where the sun shined a good part of the day. She dealt with furnishing the house, buying curtains and carpets, and giving the finishing touches that would make the house a home for Leo didn't have much time to help her.
She particularly enjoyed getting the baby's room ready. Since they didn't want to know if were expecting a baby girl or a boy, she chose neutral colors for decoration

with cream and light yellow as predominant tones. They also had a good number of teddy bears and all other kind of toy animals in all sizes, most of them gifts from Leo's comrades.

When everything was ready halfway through the pregnancy, they moved into the new house; or rather, she moved. He continued coming only on weekends for a couple of months. Not that Leo liked the idea of her alone in the house, but her mother and sisters went to visit and dine with her during the week and kept an eye on her.

The pregnancy had not been easy. Although the morning nausea was over, she felt so tired she had to shorten the workdays from the sixth month onwards, and suspend it entirely from the seventh month.

Doctors recommended her complete rest for the satisfactory ending up of the pregnancy, and she wanted that baby so badly that stood without a single objection to the soporific sessions of daily resting in bed. During that time she probably read more books that she had read in her entire life. She didn't have anything to do and had put so much weight that could hardly move alone.

She felt heavy and clumsy, but she endured the situation without a single complaint. When Leo was finally transferred he used to prepare dinner and take it on a tray to the bed where the two of them ate together. She only got up from bed to go to the toilet and Leo didn't know how she was able to withstand being held in the room twenty-four hours a day.

The time was eloping very slowly. It seemed that the expecting months didn't elapse and pregnancy would never end.

She had just fallen asleep when she felt a sharp pain that rendered her momentarily breathless. She still had almost two full weeks to go, but at this time knew she wouldn't reach the end. She tried to calm down and think serenely; didn't want to scare Leo.

She wasn't sure what to do; didn't believe the child would be born immediately. She knew that the first delivery could take hours and didn't want to spend all that time waiting at the hospital.

However, at four in the morning she was compelled to wake him up. The pain she felt was unbearable and fear oppressed her.

She was covered in sweat and trembling, writhing in pain; looked like a scared girl younger than she was.

Leo drove her to the hospital through the deserted streets at breakneck speed ignoring the red traffic lights. When they came into the emergency room, she was sat in a wheelchair and immediately taken inside.

The time she spent alone in the examination room until Leo returned from parking the car and check her in seemed to be endless. She was connected to various electronic devices to check the blood oxygenation, blood pressure, baby's heart rate and power of contractions. They were performing all kinds of procedures on her; she felt like a monkey or a guinea pig. Leo found her near hysteria, making tremendous efforts not to cry and maintain some of her self control.

The night passed slowly with the nurses and midwife in and out of the room, and the day was even harder. They had been almost twenty-four hours in the hospital and she was exhausted. In a desperate attempt to do something to release the pain that was killing her, Leo talked to the doctor to see if they could carry out a caesarean section, but so far he rejected the possibility and told him to keep calmed. Apparently everything was under control.

He was starting to get really panicky and she was beginning to despair when finally at two in the morning she was taken to the delivery room.

Having the little baby in her arms made all the last hours suffering magically disappeared. Leo watched them both ecstatic; it was hard to believe that everything had finally finished.

The arrival of Alba had caught them by surprise, but she filled their lives with satisfaction. It was the culmination of their love. Alba had come into the world on a rainy evening in May. She was born with her eyes opened, and she hadn't closed them since. Everything amazed and surprised her; she wanted to learn and experience it all.

After the birth of her little girl, she left her job and devoted herself entirely to take care of her daughter and husband. Things had not been easy, but Leo was promoted and the pay rise came handy to cover the new expenses. Neither of them wanted to borrow money from their families. Leo was strong enough to work and support them economically. She had offered to continue working part-time but he rejected the idea.

When Alba was four years old and started going to school, Leo suggested she could establish herself independently and work from home. At the beginning she didn't have many customers, but gradually word spread and she managed to gather a portfolio of clients, mainly small businesses in need of legal advice.

Soon things started to improve and for the first time they could go on holidays together. They traveled to New York in June.

She would never forget the smile in Alba's face with her eyes wide open looking up to see the skyscrapers. And her laughter when they roamed around Central Park in a chaise pulled by horses. They visited the statue of liberty, went up to the Empire State and did everything expected the tourists to do. They had such a great time.

It had taken them nearly seven years to go on honeymoon, but it was worth it. And it was even better because Alba had been with them. The girl spent all summer talking to her friends about the trip and showing the pictures to anyone who liked to take a look at them.

CHAPTER 2

"Alba, please finish your breakfast. We're gonna be late for school".
As the girl finished the toasts and cereals, she took the clean pots and plates from the dishwasher, finished collecting the dry clothes and did as much as she could of the rest of the house chores in the short time she had. She took advantage of every spare minute for she wanted to make sure she had time for more important things like being with her family.
She loved her work; did enjoy it. And she also liked to take care of her daughter and house personally. But all of this required a lot of time and dedication. It didn't matter that she got up when Leo did; she didn't stop until she was going out the door with Alba on the way to the school, and continued with the tasks as soon as she was back.
She did nearly the impossible to be able to spend some time with her daughter and husband. She waited until the girl was put to bed to clear the table from dinner, do the

washing up, clean the house and everything that needed to be done. Leo also helped her as much as he could.

Sometimes felt that she didn't spend enough quality time with them, particularly with her husband; she was always rushing. But she tried to compensate them on weekends. Neither of them complained, but sometimes she felt guilty, especially with Alba. The girl would grow soon; Alba would not be a little girl much longer, and she was afraid of wasting those precious years that would never return.

"Are you going to pick me up today, mummy?" -the girl asked while she was buckling the car safety belt.

"No, honey. Don't you remember you're going to Elise's birthday today? Her mother will collect you from the school and daddy will fetch you later when the party is finished".

"Oh, yeah. I forgot. Today is Eli's party" -Alba was excited. She had been talking about the event all week. Elise's birthday was on Tuesday, but Friday was chosen to celebrate a small party with her friends. Elise's mother had offered to pick her up from the school along with other friends to avoid the parents a trip to collect their kids.

"Mummy, mummy, can I sleep in her house tonight? Eli told me that I could stay at home all night. Anne and Louise are going to staying there. Let me stay. Please..."

"Some other time, sweetie. Daddy will pick you up later".

"Oh mum, you never let me sleep at my friends'!"

"Well, I promise you next time we'll arrange it for you to stay. Or even better, your friends could come home and sleep over" -while she knew that the girl would be in good hands at her friends' house, she didn't like to lose full sight of her at dawn for more than a few hours.

"Fine" -she said with a sigh of resignation. Alba wasn't very convinced, but for the moment she could do nothing about it-. "Why don't you come to fetch me, mummy?"

"I'm sorry, honey; I have to finish a job. It is very important that I finish it on time; otherwise my client will get very annoyed and he might not pay me".

"Will he be mad at you?"

"He will if I don't deliver it on time".

"Oh, I see. It's like when I don't do my homework and the teacher get angry with me, right? You mean something like this, mummy?"

"Yes, something like this".

The girl seemed to be abided by the explanation and changed the topic. She went on talking about her friend's birthday and making plans to arrange the sleep over at home one of these days until they reached the school.

Upon arrival they found other classmates and Alba gave her a kiss and went cheerfully with them to class waving goodbye from the entrance.

She observed her chatting with her friends, dressed in the school uniform. She wore her hair in a high ponytail adorned with a pink flower. Alba turned around and smiled at her before disappearing through the door.

That was the last time she saw her daughter alive. The next time she set eyes on her, she was on a stainless steel table, pale, motionless, lost forever. Her hair was tousled and messy and full of blood, and her beautiful pink flower was gone. Her uniform was also gone. Her clothes had been removed and she rested with her eyes closed on the cold steel table. Her little girl was very pale and she thought that she might feel very cold.

CHAPTER 3

"Am I intruding?"
For a moment it looked like she couldn't understand the words; as if she wasn't even able to see him. Slowly, her eyes lost in the immensity focused on him.
"I beg your pardon?
"What were you thinking? You were completely gone; you've not even been aware I'd returned" -the man offered her hot black coffee in a plastic cup. She took the cup and he served more coffee in another cup leaving the flask on the floor.
"Sorry, I hadn't noticed you" -she looked at the cup holding it with both hands to get warm. It was a cold morning.
"What were you thinking?" -He asked again gently.
"I was thinking in the last time I saw my daughter".
"Do you have a daughter?"
"I do... I don't... I did" -hesitated in the answer.

An immense sorrow took over her face, a pity that filled her soul and he could feel through the distance between them as a thick smoke stretching around.
"You had? How come?"
"She's gone. She is with her father".
"Do you miss her?"
"Terribly".
"How old is she?"
"Eight this year".
"Do you see her often?"
"No".
"Why not?"
"I can't. It's not possible".
"Doesn't her father allow you to see her?" -He didn't mean to interfere in her affairs, but he was intrigued. Perhaps that explained why she was there, although it seemed a bit extreme. He could image the uneasiness she felt, but surely there was some other solution to her problem. Something could be done, no doubt. The road she was taking seemed to be quite drastic. She must be certainly desperate for not been able to see another way out other than embrace the decision she had taken. Perhaps she had reached her limit of discouragement.
Either way, it didn't really mattered the reason. However, since they were both there and everything pointed out that for the same purpose, he couldn't find any wrongdoing in satisfying his curiosity. After all, it was the last opportunity for both of them to communicate with another human being.
She smiled reluctantly; a smile that didn't reach her eyes, though. He didn't understand anything. Of course, why should he? People knew nothing of her or her

tragedy. For her there was nothing more important in her life, she couldn't forget as much as she tried, but it wasn't written all over her face after all. People couldn't guess just by looking at her.

And she didn't talk about that. She never spoke of that. Not even with her family. It had been a year without mentioning that, without talking about anything; without seeing anyone; not really. Locked up at home with her grief; crying until there were no more tears left; plunged into an endless despair; wrapped up in the most absolute darkness; besieged by the absence and silence. Wishing to lose her memory and surrounded by memories that threatened to suffocate her, she was been consumed slowly, like a candle. But that fading wasn't fast enough. She wanted to blow the candle and extinguish the flame forever. There was nothing to illuminate now; only emptiness, silence, death and desolation.

"She is gone; both of them are gone; dead".

She was astonished to hear her own voice; surprised of the words that came out of her mouth. It was the first time she said it out loud. So far she hadn't been able to admit it. Dead. That word didn't exist in her vocabulary. Their loved ones were gone. They had departed. They had left her alone. But they had not died. She never said that they were dead. That part was better forgotten.

Until that very moment.

She was looking at him while speaking, but didn't see him. She was lost in a remote space; lost in the faraway distance of time.

"I'm sorry. I know that doesn't help, but I am really very sorry".

She stared at him, seeing him really for the first time since he had returned. Warmth and compassion filled his eyes.

She nodded thanking him.

"What happened?"

It was a simple question. What happened? So far, no one had dared to ask that question. Her family was worried about her, and they chose to ignore what happened; they preferred she forget what had happened. They didn't talk about it. At least, they didn't talk in front of her. Probably they didn't even spoke about it themselves, either; they were in denial. They thought that refusing to talk about it would help them and help her coping with the death of her loved ones. Maybe they were wrong.

What happened? Why remember it? It was better to ignore it. Leave it aside. Forget to mention it.

That was what everyone had done, her parents and Leo's, her siblings and in-laws. Everyone. Everybody preferred to forget. Initially, they didn't mention Leo or Alba for fear that she might collapsed; to avoid hindering her precarious improvement. She had spent a week crying, and another two more months locked at home not wanting to see anybody or talk to anyone. Finally her father had brought a professional to help her cope with the loss.

The loss! Such a nice euphemism! *The loss* were Leo and Alba. That was what she had lost, what she would never recover. That was what nobody could give her back.

The psychiatrist prescribed her some pills that left her stunned all day. She didn't crying, but she was unable to get off the couch. At the end, she decided that it was best to discard the pills and doctors, and leave her family to believe that she was surpassing the pain. That way they would leave her alone and in peace with her grief.

And so they did. Everyone believed that she was feeling better; that she had begun to accept *the loss* and could go on with her life. That was what she had led them to believe. And they had left her untroubled. And they never mentioned Leo or Alba in her presence, as if they believed that she would forget about them too.

"They had an accident. A driver didn't stop in a red traffic light and collided with them. He got away fine; not a single scratch".

He took the cup she still held in her shaking hands and stroked the back of one of them.

"I'm sorry" -he said again.

She looked at him with an immense pain reflected in her face. His expression revealed a great tenderness and understanding that touched her devastated heart.

"Would you like to tell me what happened?"

Suddenly the words started to flow from her mouth. A voice that didn't seem to be her own began to speak. And nothing could stop her. All those months with hidden, silent memories... now the silence was replaced by an endless verbiage.

She told him about her life, about Leo, about Alba, about herself. She told him everything she felt when she had her daughter in her arms for the first time, when she began to walk and talk, the first day she went to school, and many more details that she had almost forgotten; or rather that had disallowed to remember.

She described to him the life that she'd shared with them, their dreams, Leo's love for life, the willing to create a better future for her daughter. She portrayed Leo and Alba and the life they had in such a way that he felt he already knew them without having ever met them.

"I said goodbye and saw her going into the school. I always waited there until she was gone inside. I saw her off and I left".

Tears were falling now like a torrent down her face.

"That day she was going to a friend's birthday party and her father was going to fetch her. I should have gone myself. I should have been with her rather than finish a stupid project that had to present the next day to a client. The funny part is that I didn't hand over the work after all and lost the customer anyway".

Paul listened in silence while an unbalanced and unhealthy laughter emerged from the woman's throat. She finally calmed down and continued with her remorseful tale.

"She wanted to sleep over in her friend's house; other girls were going to do it. But I didn't allow her; I wanted her at home. It was Friday and I loved waking up on Saturday and prepare breakfast. We all sat at the table and talked. During the week we had no time; Leo left before us and we always left in a hurry, so we couldn't sit down and have breakfast and talk placidly. We did that on the weekends".

He listened to her without saying a word. He was still holding her hand, now firmly.

"Leo went to picked her up around seven. He had helped me to set the table for dinner. We had prepared some pretty floral decorations with daisies; they were Alba's favorite flowers" -she wiped with the sleeve the tears that had slipped down her neck-. "Leo could have left a few minutes earlier had I not asked him to help me set the table. The two of them would be alive had I not been so selfish". -Paul could feel the torment that humbled her soul, the torture of her shrunken heart-. "Two policemen came home at eight. They told me there had been a terrible accident. My husband and my daughter… They knew who they were by the photograph Leo had in his wallet and his driving license, but someone had to identify them. They asked if some relative could go to recognize the corpses. That's how I got the news… I guess for them they were only two more casualties. Routine. Another job before the end of the workday; just breaking the news to the widow. But for me they weren't just another victims of a tragedy; they were much more than that. They were my whole life" -she distilled sadness throughout her pores. Her hand was frozen.

He kept quiet. He understood she wanted to talk; she had to talk about it. He knew very well how she felt. Once the gate of the emotion was opened, you had to leave all the water out. It couldn't be stopped. It was not humanly possible to stop the flood that had been contained for so long.

"I didn't want anybody with me. I didn't want anyone to see them. They were mine. It was my last chance to be with them" -the tears ran down her cheeks and the suffering that oppressed not only her throat but her spirit was palpable.

Listening to her he could feel her pain as his own.

"I cannot avoid thinking that it was my fault. Would had I allowed her to sleep over at her friend's this would have not happened; Leo wouldn't had gone to collect her. Or had he left a few minutes earlier, that car that didn't stop at the red traffic light would not have clashed with them. Now they would be alive" -she sobbed uncontrollably.

"It wasn't your fault. You didn't make the car skip the red light" -he hugged her closer against his chest while she cried convulsively. They spent a good while like that until she calmed down and began to sob quietly.

He was still holding her in his strong arms when she raised her head and looked at him with eyes flooded with tears but comforted.

It was like she was observing things from a different perspective for the first time. Suddenly a light arose in the sky in the middle of the storm. It wasn't her fault. It was not her fault. She wasn't guilty for the car that hadn't stopped at the red traffic light.

"It wasn't my fault -it was barely a whisper".

"No, it wasn't. You've been blaming yourself all this time, haven't you?"

"Yes. I think the guilt was even more painful that having lost them both" -she looked at him and smiled through the tears-. "Thank you".

"Why you thank me?"

"Because you have opened my eyes. You have given me the peace that I had lost when I lost them. Somehow you have brought them back to me".

"Sometimes there's nothing like opening your heart to a stranger to feel better".

"You're right. My family has been trying to help me all this time, but the only thing I've done has been set them aside and isolate myself from them. I think they believe the person they knew wasn't there anymore. I thought so, too".

"Don't you think so now?"

"No. I think I've returned. I'm back to reality; I'm back to life. I will never be the same I was before, but at least I won't be the ghost of myself I've been lately. And I owe you that much".

"So, you're not jumping?"

She parted from him and approached the edge to look at the black water that ran under the bridge. She considered it for a while before answering.

"I think not. Maybe I can learn to live with myself now".

"That's an excellent idea, mate" -there was no wit but sadness in his remark this time.

He stared at her with his hands tucked in his pockets while she remained absentminded contemplating the abyss that loomed beneath.

She seemed so young and helpless. And he had seen so much pain and suffering in her eyes... for the first time in a very long time someone had managed to enter his heart, not only the beating muscle nested in his chest but his deepest core, and shake him.

He wondered why there was so much grief in this world; how was possible that human beings inflicted so much pain to themselves. As if life itself didn't already do enough damage to them, they seemed to revel in the sadness and despair as if they felt a sordid and nostalgic gratification in abandon and condemn themselves to an eternal despair.

But in this very moment he was pleased to have put his two cents to the pile and helped to alleviate that pain; at least, her pain. And she was the only person in the world who mattered to him here and now.

But helping others, he knew, was always easier.

The desperation of the woman had nested so deep inside him as nothing else has done in a very long time. Her tears had stung the hard shell that covered his heart and she had managed to pass the armor that he had forged around his soul. He had isolated himself from the world long ago. He had continued breathing air, feeding his hunger and filling his emptiness with a frenetic pace of work without satisfying his soul. Nothing had been able to overcome the iron shielding of his hostility towards the world. No one had conveyed the animosity he felt for life, which had deprived him of the most valuable thing he had.

Everybody had finally ditched him. He had been left with his ghosts. And it was better that way; he felt better that way. Alone; with no one around who mattered to him. No one to cause that sharp pain that people you love unleashed when they leave you. He didn't cared for nothing and no one; nobody even distracted the wreck of feelings he had drifted through unknown seas.

A ship that many people considered already sunk.

He only cared about his work; that was the only thing that kept him alive. He didn't work to live anymore; now he lived to work. The work was the only thing that gave him satisfaction; the unique satisfaction he allowed himself in life.

The woman turned towards him. She had large green bright eyes. Eyes that reminded him other eyes he knew so well long ago.

CHAPTER 4

"Here will be the kitchen, and there the lounge" -Paul explained moving from side to side covering with his hands the empty space between the chalk-lines marked on the ground.
Julia smiled happily watching his enthusiasm and made fun of it.
"Why do we want a kitchen for? I can't cook".
"You don't need to cook. I'll hire a chef to prepare supper every day; and a butler to serve us dinner at candlelight every night. Then, we'll drink brandy sitting in front of the fireplace".
"You have everything planned, don't you?"
"Absolutely everything. When the children arrive we will hire a babysitter to take care of them while you keep painting. You'll do lots of portraits of all of them and fill the house with the pictures hanging on the walls".
"And exactly how many children will we have?" -there was a tinge of fun irony in her voice
"Five or six, at least".

Julia raised her eyebrows.

"Wouldn't I have something to say about it?"

"You'll be so happy that you'll look forward to have more" -he approached and kissed her passionately.

They were going to get married and he was showing her on the field the house he was building for them. As architect, that was his best work so far, wanted everything to be perfect. He had not left the minor detail in the design to chance; nor had he spared expenses.

He was a prestigious architect when he met her through a job that her father had entrusted him. Every time he had come to show her dad the plans, he had seen her dressed in old clothes covered in paint. She had introduced herself. Julia was like that. Unlike her sister, who he had also met in the working visits, Julia had a cheerful and carefree character, and loved to meet people. It wasn't as beautiful or has as delicate features as her sister; she was taller and always seemed to be in good form.

One day she had showed him her work while he was waiting for her father. He was amazed. The paintings were powerful; somehow, they reflected the strength and character of the artist. She also felt curious about his work, although it was something far less artistic, so Paul invited her to his studio.

Shortly after, they began dating and six months later he asked her to marry him.

Everything had happened very quickly. His friends mocked him for having finally found the woman who made him want to tie the knot, something he used to swear would never happen.

"The woman able to catch me hasn't been born yet" -he used to say.

But Julia attracted him at first sight. She trapped his heart with her humanity and tenderness, and his brain with her intelligence and sharpness.

They married in a civil ceremony attended only by the closest relatives. There were fifteen people in total, including them. Julia wore a blue dress and carried a bouquet of violets. Her bright blond hair tied in a low bun framed her beautiful face, and her smile illuminated everything around her.

They became husband and wife in a quick ceremony that ended with the exchange of the wedding rings and the traditional kiss. Paul couldn't wait to be alone with her, but he had to linger while they celebrated their marriage with their family in the restaurant.

For the meantime, they settled in his bachelor flat, which soon became Julia's improvised workshop. Her clothes began to fill the cupboards and her belongings were scattered throughout the apartment. Despite the prevailing chaos, Paul was thrilled to come back home every day and found her there.

They went to dine out and visit small villages on the weekends where they spent the night and enjoyed being together. Life smiled at him as it had not done before. Once the house was finished, they moved there and started putting into practice his ideas of creating a big family.

But time passed by and the children didn't come.

They went to doctors to have a whole battery of tests done. His went well; there was no problem that prevented him from having kids.

However, they discovered disappointed that Julia couldn't have children. She had to undergo numerous and annoying examinations until they found out the cause of her infertility. She had suffered an apparently asymptomatic infection as a teenager that had left her fallopian tubes filled with scar tissue and therefore, useless for conception. Not even science with all the advances could help them. The adoption was the only option they had left.

Discovering that they couldn't have children was a setback. From a rakehell running away from commitments he had grown to be a faithful and devoted husband and wished to become the dearest father of a large family.

Julia also felt disappointed, but mostly she felt she had failed him. It was a difficult time for both of them. She sank into depression and he didn't know how to help her.

But they finally overpowered it. It took time, but they succeeded. They were again the happy couple they were before. She knew he didn't blame her or was upset, but she also realized that not having children grieved him. She had seen how he looked at his own nieces and nephews and knew the pain he felt for the lack of offspring.

Yet, they had talked about it, and they had decided that the adoption was not for them. If God didn't want them to have children, Julia had said, He must have a good reason for it.

He wouldn't have minded to adopt, but Julia was determined not to. And she proved to be right.

Few months later, he got a phoned called in his study. Julia had fainted in the exposition gallery and she had been rushed to the hospital. As it happened, an apparently trivial collapse, turned into something really serious.

After a long and tedious series of tests they discovered she had a brain tumor. She couldn't undergo surgery; the prognosis wasn't good.

Chemotherapy was the only palliative treatment they could use for her. She could last six months, maybe a year if she was lucky.

It was a terrible blow for him; for both. Julia was so full of life, so joyous... it didn't seem right.

"It never is" -the doctor said when he paid him a visit. Paul wanted to talk to him, know if there was something he could do, any chance however small that was. He needed to find a hope however insignificant that could be.

But the doctor was brutal; he had already said everything. She knew it. There was nothing else to do. Just live the moment and enjoy as much as possible while she was still feeling well.

"Try to cherish life while she still preserves her understanding. Unfortunately there is nothing we can do for her. It is not possible to operate the tumor. Because of its location, we would put her life at serious risk, and it is not certain that the benefits could overcome the dangers of the surgical procedure".

"Are you sure there's nothing that can be done?"

"Of course you are free to consult other experts. But if you are going to do it, I advise you to do it quickly.

Don't waste the little remaining time she has in useless tests".

He nodded and thanked the doctor.

"I'm sorry. I wish I could give you hope, but I cannot fool you. Anyway, Julia seems to be a strong-willed woman. That helps. Sometimes people surprise us".

It was the only thing Paul could hold to. Julia's willpower and her desire to live.

He wasn't sure he wanted to know more. He knew the main thing. Julia was dying. His world was melting down. She needed him; still, he wasn't able to look at her without feeling tears in his eyes. Knowing her as he did, the last thing Julia would have liked was to inspire compassion.

And it wasn't compassion what he felt.

What he felt was a pain so intense that prevented him from breathing.

What he felt was a love as deep as he would have never thought possible to feel.

What he felt was such a terribly fear at the thought of losing her that he didn't allowed himself to even think about it.

He had to know, the doctor had told him. He had to be prepared for what was coming. It would be very hard. A time would come that it would be harder for him than for her. A time would come when she would begin to lose memory. A time would come that, perhaps, she wouldn't even recognize him.

He wanted to begin the treatment as soon as possible, but Julia insisted in traveling around. She yearns for visiting the places she had always dreamed of. She wanted to remember before forget odors from different countries, colors of different lands and aromas of exotic food.

She wanted to feel the breeze caressing her face and feel the rain drenching her body.

She wanted to bathe in the warm sea and in the cold ocean currents.

She wanted to climb mountains and cross meadows.

She wanted to live.

They were traveling for almost three months; it was the happiest time in their life.

They first took a trip to Italy. They visited the Coliseum and the Vatican; they went up to the piazza di Espagna and stopped at countless Roman churches. They threw coins in the Fontana di Trevi, as it couldn't have been otherwise, wishing as all the tourists did to come back there again. But Paul knew they would never return. And Julia knew it too. They traveled in gondola through the canals of Venice and sat down on the terraces in the piazza di San Marcos. They enjoyed the art in Florence and saw the Vesuvius in Naples. They mingled with the people; they enjoyed its gastronomy and its landscapes.

They navigated in a cruise line by the Mediterranean Sea to Malta and Crete, finishing in Greece where they visited Athens and the Parthenon and admired the remaining of the city founded so long ago. They tested the Greek food and were delighted with the typical Greek dance performed by male dancers.

They sailed the Nile in Egypt, and visited the pyramids and the Abu Simbel temple; they dived in the Red Sea and enjoyed the aquatic diversity down there. They crossed the border to Jordan and went to Petra; and later in Israel, they prayed in the wall of laments, admired the Death Sea and toured the Sacred City of Jerusalem.

Traveling through those last three countries in a row wasn't an easy task. The border security officers were suspicious when they showed their passports and they had to explain in detail who they were and what business they had there. There was always the risk of terrorists and the border police was very suspicious of tourists that crossed through their customs successively. But they managed to convince them and enter the countries, anyway. And it proved to be worth the trouble. They greatly enjoyed the visit to all these places.

They travelled by land through North Africa until reaching Morocco and then took a plane to Paris. Julia had always loved Paris. The city of light was charming. She had travel to the artists' neighbourhood when younger, and spent hours in the Louvre Museum and museum d'Orsy, visiting the multiples galleries in the city and Napoleon tomb.

However, now she could see a different aspect of Paris. Be there with Paul was by far the best experience of the city that she had never had. Now it was full of hidden meaning, romantic boat trips along the Seine and candlelight dinners on the boat restaurants lined along the River, visits to the opera and Notre Dame…

The Paris she was discovering with Paul wasn't the Paris she remembered. Now it was a magical city where she enjoyed every minute spent there, together.

They had no timetable, no plans; they went wherever they wanted to go, did whatever they feel like doing. They didn't talked about her illness; preferred to ignore it, squish it, and make it disappear; deny that exist it.

But that wasn't going to happen. Julia had started to have small lapses of memory and had lost weight. It wasn't anything spectacular, but Paul preferred not to take any risk. He wanted to come back home; wanted her to start the treatment. He craved to cling to the little hope that still remained and keep her by his side for as long as possible.

At the end she relented. They returned and she began treatment.

He knew there had been times where Julia had repented for having done it, and deep down he also regretted and blamed himself for being so selfish and wanting to hold to her at all costs.

The treatment was even harder than the disease itself. They went to the hospital twice a week and spent endless hours there waiting. Waiting to have the blood sample taken, waiting for the results, waiting to see the doctor again and had the treatment prescribed, waiting for an empty bed so she could finally have the treatment, and waiting for a taxi to take them back home.

He sat by her side while the treatment was administered to her and they chatted. Then, Julia insisted he go down to the cafeteria to eat something and he went down reluctantly, more to please her and let her rest for a while, as he knew she needed to, that because he was really hungry. He sat in the canteen quiet and crestfallen, hating being there, swallowing the tears, the rage and the pain he felt.

Then he went back with her again carrying a sandwich and a couple of coffees for both contriving dishes they had that day in the menu and described to her what he had for lunch. And Julia believed him, or so he reckoned. At the end of the long day, when they finished the treatment, they left the hospital and took a taxi to come back home.

At the beginning he drove her in his car, but it soon became apparent that it was not possible to drive and take care of her at the same time, so they used taxis. Both families had offered to drive them, but she didn't want them to be there.

She didn't covet anybody to see her like that. She didn't want anyone by her side; only him. Occasionally she spoke on the phone with them and tried to be the same happy and jolly woman she used to be, and they feigned to believe her although they knew well that she was only pretending.

When they arrived at home she was so tired after six to eight hours in the hospital that could hardly wait to lie down on the couch. And soon after, she started vomiting. It was terrible to see her like that. She bended and twisted while trying to free her stomach of the non-existent food, trying to liberate her body from the infamous toxic compound that attacked the malignant cells of her brain and also threatened to destroy the healthy ones.

And that wasn't even the worst.

The worst struck when her hair started to fall. One morning few days after the treatment had started, she was surprised to find a handful of hair after she combed, and more when she touched her head.

When Paul came to the living room she was crying quietly with the hair in her hand. He approached and hugged her, burying his face in her chest.

"Do you think I'll be pretty bald?" -Julia tried to smile.

"You'll be the prettiest hairless girl in history" -he said unable to hold back the tears that ran down his face and soaked the collar of his shirt.

After that, Julia preferred to shave her hair completely.

Her sister, in an attempt to encourage her, had suggested to buy several wigs to facilitate the possibility of drastically change her appearance every day. She could choose different hairstyles and hair colors, and Julia, flaunting her old sense of humor, had followed the joke pretending to consider other bizarre options such as a blue or a pink wig. But she really didn't want to wear hairpieces. She said it would make her illness even more obvious. Instead she used a bandanna knotted at the neck at home and for going to the hospital. She was very pretty. The lack of hair only highlighted even more her beautiful features.

Only in the evenings the scarf was removed and she left her bald head free. They switched off the light and Paul cuddled her in bed. And they spent the night that way. Sometimes they talked for hours; neither of them slept much.

He gave up his job to devote himself exclusively to her. He wanted to spend every day, every minute she had left by her side.

The treatment left her exhausted. She was so tired that Paul had to pick her up in his arms to take her upstairs to the bedroom.

His life was reduced to the four walls of the house and the hospital. He didn't see anyone, except doctors and nurses; didn't left home except to take her to the hospital.

Julia's parents, not to mention his own family, were almost as concerned about him as they were about her. They knew how much he loved her, and how difficult was going to be for him when she wasn't there. But they were not expecting him to bury himself with her as he seemed to be doing.

"Paul, this is terrible but you have to be strong" -his father had told him one of the times they had visited them when he saw him so emaciated-. "I'm sure Julia wouldn't want you to give up. You have to take care of yourself and move on, son".

It was one of the few times he had admitted defeat. He had wept like a child in the garage in his father's arms while his mother accompanied Julia. He couldn't even start to imagine life without her.

Julia began to worsen in September. At the beginning it was only trivial things. She forgot a phone number, when they talked about someone she knew only too well couldn't match the face with the name, and even mixed family members and called them by other's names.

The doctor said the tumor had begun to affect major parts of the brain. Chemotherapy had a limited effect; it could not do more. From that moment on, she would go from bad to worse. Paul had to be prepared for what was coming.

And what came was horrible.

Seeing her deteriorate physically was bad enough, but seeing her lose her memory was something even worse to endure. And he couldn't imagine anything worse than what she had already experienced.

She still had many lucid moments in which Paul sat on the couch holding her in his arms and they talked for hours. They talked about the past, dreams they had, and fantasies they shared when they started their life together. They talked about her family, too. She told him stories of her as a little girl, the mischief and the naughty things she and her sister used to do when they were younger.

Sometimes they spoke about the future, although Paul was very reluctant to talk about it.

"Paul, you have to move on, for me, for both of us".

"I don't want to think about that. I can't imagine life without you".

"It is regrettable that we have only been together for such a short time, but I cherish those moments as the best in my life. I wouldn't like to think I caused you so much pain that shuttered your heart, my dear. I want you to remember the good times".

"I will never forget you, Julia. You're the most important person in my life. But let's not talk about that now. You are not going anywhere. I won't let you go" - he was trying to tease her, but even to him it sounded fake.

She stroked his cheek and looked him in the eyes.

"I'm dying. The end is near. It's closer than we think".

"No, I won't let you go" -he refused to accept the reality.

"Paul, you know that I have to go. I would prefer not have to do it. I wish I could stay; there's nothing I would like more than that. I would give anything for staying here with you" -tears rolled down her face; her beautiful face. That face he had come to love so much.

They both wept hugging each other, knowing they were probably enjoying one of the last clear moments of her.

"You have to promise me something".

"Anything you want".
"No, listen. This is important to me".
"What do you want me to promise?"
"I want you to promise me you're going to be fine".
"Julia..."
"No, really. Promise me you will take care of yourself. Promise me you're going to move forward".

He didn't want to lie to her; didn't know what he was going to do without her. But it seemed important for her to believe he would be okay when she was gone.

"Okay, Julia. I promise I will take care of myself, I promise I will move forward" -he had never felt such a miserable liar as he felt at the moment.

He didn't know what he was going to do when she was gone. He didn't want to carry on without her by his side. There would be nothing to live for.

But he had to lie for her; he had to give her the last moments of peace. He owes her that much. She must have the opportunity to leave in peace, without worrying about him, and felt that was the only thing he could do for her now.

"I have always thought you would make a good father. You must give yourself the opportunity when I'd gone" -she said in a soft and tired voice.

"No, I can't think of anything like that Julia. If I haven't had children with you, I don't want them with anyone else".

"Paul... how do you think I feel for denying you the possibility of having kids? How do you think I feel just leaving you so lonely?" -She put her fingers on his lips to avoid him to reply-. "I want you to live a full life when I'm gone. I don't want you to shut yourself to the world only because of what happened to me".

He had never met someone as gutsy as her. He didn't know how he would have reacted if things would have been the other way around. He would have probably sunk, would have been bitter with life, with God, with all.

He wasn't even sure he believed in God. He had never been very religious, although he wouldn't have minded to get married in the Church. They were married in a civil ceremony instead because Julia had insisted. With the exception of the touristic visits during their last trip together, he had only trampled a church on the occasions he couldn't avoid, which were weddings, baptisms and funerals. Only these.

Julia wasn't too religious either, but since she had learned she was sick had started to attend church regularly. She didn't take notice of the mass; she only came to pray. She sat on a bench and seemed to detach herself completely from reality. It was almost as if she could hear God.

Sometimes he accompanied her, and others he sat down at the end of the church looking at her. He had even come to feel jealous watching her flushed, praying with that expression of ecstasy on her face. It was almost as if she was thanking God.

At the beginning he also prayed. He prayed for her to be healed. He prayed they were wrong in the diagnosis. He prayed for her to continue much longer at his side.

But no one listened to him.

When she began to worsen and still went to church he didn't pray any more. He hated whoever was up there, if it happens to be someone.

He didn't understand what comfort she could find in there. How could she believe and pray to someone that by all means had forsaken her?

But Julia seemed to like going there, she found peace and comfort; and for him that was enough, even though he had to do increasingly more efforts not to cry out to that God who had abandoned them, who was so cruelly punishing them.

In the middle of November, they had to take her into hospital. It was no longer possible for him to take care of her alone. Her health had deteriorated so much that it was hard to breathe and her kidneys had stopped working. Now she spent two to three hours every other day plugged into a dialysis machine.

She forgot where she was and talked about things from the past as if they were current. She told the nurses she was going to get married and some days even said it to him when she took him for one of the doctors.

She had already scarce clear moments; spent much of the day sleeping and Paul remained sitting by her side, holding her hand or caressing her fingers. Most of the time she wasn't aware of that.

One night in early December he woke up and saw her looking at him and smiling, although he wasn't sure if she recognized him.

"I love you" -she said-. "Thank you for giving me so much. For having been by my side all this time. Now I have to go. But I needed to tell you; I wanted you to know it. I don't want you to be sad when I'd gone".

She spoke slowly but calmly in a soft voice and didn't take her eyes of him.

He approached the bed and took her hands. He took them up to his lips and kissed them as tears wet what other time had been a smooth and soft girly skin, and was now dry and rumple crust.

The disturbance didn't let him breathe, he felt gassed. There were so many things he wanted to say to her. So many things he wanted to thank her for. So many things he still wanted to share with her.

"I love you" -he said that much. There was no need for more. She already knew it.

She granted him a last smile; then closed her eyes and departed in silence.

Paul sensed the flaccid lifeless hand that squeezed between his. She had a peaceful expression in her face. He couldn't but thank her for the last lucid moments she had shared with him and for having said goodbye. He would always remember it.

He didn't know how long remained there, alone, next to her, bathed in silent tears. His soul determined to die with her, but his body stubbornly continued breathing.

When the nurse came into the room and realized she had died she left discreetly to tell the doctor. There was nothing else to do for her, except certify her death. They had expected it for days. She looked at the clock to record the time of death. She was used to see death almost every day on the guard where she worked, but the deep love the man had shown for the woman wasn't something she saw every day. She felt a knot in her throat and had to wait a few moments to recover before was able to do her job.

They accompanied him to a room and offered him coffee; and saved him the pain of having to tell the family. The hospital had her parent's phone number, and they took care of everything.

The rest that went on the next couple of days he barely noticed. The cemetery was full of people, there were lots of flowers from all their friends and people he didn't know.

Standing next to the tomb, with Julia's parents on one side and his on the other, he felt like an orphan; orphan of love, orphan of life, orphan of her. He hardly sensed the thin and cold rain that soaked him to the bone.

As they lowered the coffin he could see her in his mind, cheerful, laughing; the Julia he knew and loved. That wasn't the woman who was now been buried. He felt that Julia wasn't there and that helped him to overcome the moment.

Her mother was crying now in distress clung to her husband and her other daughter, who couldn't restrain her emotion.

Then, they went to the Church. There would be a mass for her. The temple was packed; there were as many people as in the cemetery if no more. He was sitting in the first bench, the one reserved for the family, but he scarcely noticed who was by his side.

The priest dedicated some praise to her during the ceremony. She had been a good wife, a good daughter, a good sister, a good friend for her friends, and a good God-fearing Christian.

He was about to laugh hearing that. What the hell mattered if she had been a God-fearing Christian? What kind of God could rejoice in inflicting pain that way?

What kind of God could have given her to him, bring her to his life and then take her away from him?

Then the priest offered him his condolences and so did everyone that had come to the Church. He greeted them without seeing them. He accepted the condolences of anyone who approached him and gave him a hand-shake. It was a never-ending day, and however passed in a blink of an eye.

His parents volunteered to stay with him for a few days or to take him with them until he felt better. But he preferred to be alone; in his house; in the house he shared with her for just six years. He wanted to be alone with his memories; alone with his grief; alone with his loss.

He came into the room and laid on the bed he shared with Julia. In good and bad, in health and sickness, until death parted them. And death had separated them.

He stayed awake until dawn, recalling forgotten moments, remembering every instant lived with her. When at last he fell asleep, he continued dreaming about her. And he woke up feeling her by his side.

The reality broke through between the fog and he recalled that Julia was no longer with him. The pain seized him and he wept. He wept like a child. He wept for the moments lived together and for those he would never live with her. He cried for her and cried for himself. He cried because she was gone and cried because he had to stay.

He cried until he had no more tears left.

Julia's parents called him in the beginning to take interested in him. They invited him for dinner and to visit them. But he avoided them invariably and they ended up letting him alone.

The same thing happened with everyone else. No one could cross the wall of isolation that he had created around him. And they began to move away and leave him alone.

That was what he wanted. He couldn't cope with the company of anybody around. He had become what Julia had wanted so keenly to avoid. He took shelter in his work and recovered more than enough the time lost over the previous months that had spent with her.

And he forgot.

He forgot how to live, but not how to breathe. He forgot how to laugh. He forgot how to enjoy. He even forgot that once he was alive and had loved.

Over time he had learned so well how to pretend to be alive that those who didn't know him well believed him to be an insolent cynic devoid of feelings.

He had raised a wall to protect himself from feeling, a wall that separated him from everything and everyone. Nothing could tear down this wall; nobody could trespass it. It became the only thing protecting him, the only thing separating him from madness.

In a month time, it would be the fourth anniversary of Julia's death. He had tried to move forward as she had asked him to do, but could no longer carry on with his life. The emptiness he felt in his soul was widening increasingly and threatened to become infinite. The self-imposed lack of human warmth froze his heart and his loneliness was heavier every day. He had reached his limit.

He had already spent a long time without a reason for living, with no reason to go on, and the prospect of facing another Christmas with memories flooding his mood had became unbearable.

CHAPTER 5

His stranger companion approached him and caressed his cheek. He was startled for a moment. It was such a familiar gesture to him. He had forgotten she was by his side at the bridge.
"Do you really want to end?"
She said it with a soft voice full of tenderness. She seemed younger than before. It looked like relishing the ghosts would have taken away years from her.
He wondered how old she was; must have asked it out loud because she answered.
"Thirty-four".
"You are about her age when I met her".
"Was she pretty?"
"Very much; as pretty as you are. She had large green eyes, like yours. But she was taller; almost as much as me".
Despite the smile in his lips, a deep grief overshadowed his eyes.

"Did you love her so much?" -It was a simple question, made with much tenderness and understanding.

"More than I ever imagined possible. However, sometimes I have come to hate her for leaving me".

"Did she dump you?"

"This is an understatement. She died of a brain tumor almost four years ago".

"I'm sorry".

He nodded accepting her sympathy as she had done before.

"I'm sure she would have liked to stay with you".

"She was such a happy girl... never complained; not even at the end. She accepted everything as if it was a divine commandment".

"Maybe it was. Perhaps everything that happens to us has a purpose after all".

"She would have said the very same thing".

"Was it very hard at the end?" -she felt a tremendous empathy for this stranger who had returned her to life. She needed to understand him, to know what had led him to this situation. She started to believe that perhaps there was a reason for them to have met there.

He had saved her. Perhaps she could save him, too. Perhaps the gods had conspired together to save them both; for one to save the other.

"It was terrible. The last few weeks she was just a shadow of herself".

"Have you been by her side throughout that time?"

"Yes; since she was diagnosed".

"How long did she last?"

Coming from anyone else, he would have taken it as an insult. But he realized there wasn't any kind of morbid feeling in her. He talked about Julia's death as she had spoken of her husband's and daughter's death. Both shared the experience of having lost a loved one in very difficult circumstances. There weren't any malicious intentions in her questions.

It was quite the opposite, really. He appreciated that answering her questions, talking about Julia, relieved him. He started to experience gratifying warmth in his heart to remember. He began to realize that the walls that had created to protect himself, to stop the pain of having lost Julia and also to save him from madness, were beginning to crumble.

"They predicted from six months to a year. She lasted eleven months. The last few days she hardly acknowledged me; spent most of the time sleeping".

She listened in silence, as if she was his therapist. But in contrast to these professionals, the woman responded to his feelings, she didn't restrain herself to listen indifferently. She exuded friendliness and cordiality.

"Only at the end she recovered her judgment for a few minutes".

"And you were with her in those last minutes?" -she said it almost more as a statement than as a question.

"Yes. I will never forget it. They were the worst and the best moments at the same time".

"You don't know how I envy you! At least you could say goodbye. I wasn't that lucky".

"But the end is the same. She also left".

"Yes, but at least you have the comfort of having seen her leave, you've been with her. You could say goodbye".

"Yes, that's true".

They were both leaning on the hand-rail of the bridge, looking down, each one lost in their own thoughts. They felt like two old friends reunited after a long time and become acquaintance with their current lives.

Paul felt that the woman beside him that was going to share his same fate few minutes ago had gotten him out of his isolation. She had made him cross the bridge he was afraid of and yet hadn't become crazy, as he feared. In fact, he felt free; and alive.

"For a long time I hated her for leaving me. I know that it was ridiculous, she was not to blame, but I hated her for willingly accept what was happening to her. I thought she should have rebelled".

"I also hated them. I hated Leo, really". -And she continued with the explanation-. "I hated him for having been with my daughter in the last moments of her life. I hated him for being lucky enough to walk away with her. I hated him for leaving me alone and not even give me the opportunity to say goodbye. I hated him because it was him who collected Alba instead of me. It should have been me; I should have been in the car instead of him. Thus, I could have gone with my little girl rather than stay here" -despite her words, there was no hatred in her expression; only grief and deep pain; and also a feeling of release. The torment she had endured last year referred.

"We have spent too much time hating and forgetting. Instead we should have focused on remembering and therefore move on and leave the ghosts behind".

"But, remembering that we'd loved them wouldn't make us feel even more the loss of our loved ones?" -the woman asked.

"Remember means accept that we were fortunate enough to have had them in our lives and have been loved. We should have remembered that they hadn't left voluntarily; they hadn't deserted us. Simply, they had no choice".

"And we could finally forgive ourselves for been alive".

"Yes; we could stop punishing us for being alive. And who knows? Maybe even give us another chance in life" -he reflected.

"Do you think we are still on time?" -her hand quivered when she put it on his arm.

"It's never too late for a last chance, or so they say".

"Then, you are not you going to jump?"

The smile came first to his eyes.

"I think I would like to go with you for a coffee somewhere. Mine is already cold".

"And it isn't too good, either. And the sugar is missing".

"I'm sorry, madam. Next time I plan to jump from a bridge I'll take special care to prepare a good coffee. You never know when you are going to find a prudish travel companion" -he said as he offered her his arm with an eloquent invitation.

She held his arm as she bowed to him.

"What about some muffins to go with? I forgot to take them when I prepared the coffee this morning".

"That would be nice; I didn't had breakfast today. But I prefer donuts, if you don't mind".

"Any special requirements, madam?" -He asked amused.

"Chocolate ones, please. I like chocolate" -the woman smiled in a naughty way and Paul felt that warmth began to nest again in his heart.

"Humm, you have a sweet tooth".

He looked at the watch. They had been talking more than three hours. Possibly..., no, surely this woman had saved his life; and he didn't only meant he was still alive. She had saved him from his particular hell he had locked himself in.

"Not sure we can find a place where they still serve breakfast, it's a little late. But we can try".

She checked her watch and seemed surprised to see how much time they had been talking.

"I cannot believe we've been here for hours!"

"Well, if we don't find a cafe where breakfast is served, we can go to my place. I prepare great toasts; I also have croissants if you prefer them. You are more than welcome to come".

"Do you have all that?"

"Yes. I left them ready for when they came to my house after the funeral".

"Are you serious?"

"Of course I am".

"My God! You thought everything throughout. I don't even know what I have in the fridge. I didn't do any arrangement for my funeral. Next time I will take it into account".

They both laughed out loud.

"No; I think there will be no more funerals for the moment. What say you?"

"I think you're right. There are still many things to live for".

They began to walk hand in hand towards the end of the bridge where they had come from.

"By the way, what's your name?"

"Theresa".

"Theresa, I like that name. I think this could be the start of a new beginning for the two of us".

And holding each other's hand, they walked off the bridge engaged in an exciting conversation. They were two people who had returned to life.

Who knew what the future could bring them?

If you can dream it, you can do it

-Walt Disney-

Made in the USA
Charleston, SC
02 November 2015